D0956028

THIS
BOOK
BELONGS
TO:
gunnison county
Libraries
connect.   discover.   imagine.   learn.

SPIRIT TOTEMS

CHRISTOPHER E. LONG
&
MICHAEL GEIGER

When adventure is your destination!

Boston • Denver • Los Angeles • Phoenix

Visit us online at www.actionopolis.com

ACTIONOPOLIS
Published by Komikwerks, LLC
1 Ruth Street Worcester, MA 01602

KOMIKWERKS

Created by Actionopolis, Christopher E. Long, and Michael Geiger
Based on a concept by Patrick Coyle and Shannon Eric Denton

First Edition

Printed in China.

DISTRIBUTED BY PUBLISHERS GROUP WEST

Library of Congress Cataloging-in-Publication Data
Long, Christopher E.
Blackfoot Braves Society: Spirit Totems / Christopher E. Long and Michael Geiger
p. cm. – (Blackfoot Braves Society: Spirit Totems ; 1)
Summary: Danger lurks at summer camp as three new friends stumble upon supernatural secrets.
ISBN: 0-9742803-9-9
[1. Legends–Juvenile Fiction. 2. Friendship–Juvenile Fiction.]
I. Geiger, Michael II. Title
2006902387

Other books from

• **The Anubis Tapestry** •

• **The Forest King** •

• **Heir to Fire** •

• **What I Did On My Hypergalactic Interstellar Summer Vacation** •

• **Zombie Monkey Monster Jamboree** •

And more to come!

For more information on
Blackfoot Braves Society or any of our other
exciting books, visit our website:
www.actionopolis.com

LIST of FULL PAGE ILLUSTRATIONS

To Jamie and Jackson,
for giving my life meaning.
−Christopher

I'd like to dedicate this
book to the dedicated.
− Michael

BLACKFOOT BRAVES * SOCIETY

Howling Canyons

Thunderhead
Falls

BLACKFOOT

Thunder
Trailhead

The rich kid arrived at summer camp

CHAPTER ONE
The Rich Kid

Jackson Brady sat alone in the back of the stretch limousine. He clutched his backpack to his chest and rested a hand on the suitcase lying on the seat next to him. He looked up at the chauffeur sitting behind the wheel, who happened to glance into the rearview mirror at that moment and caught him staring. Jackson quickly looked away.

"We're almost there," the chauffeur said. "About another ten minutes or so."

"Okay," Jackson mumbled. "Thanks."

Jackson had told his father over and over not to have a limousine pick him up from the airport. He had tried telling his dad how inappropriate it would be to roll into summer camp in a limo. His father had nodded like he understood completely and had muttered that he would have his secretary arrange appropriate transportation from the airport to the summer camp.

When Jackson had stepped out of his father's corporate jet and saw the chauffeur standing next to the gleaming stretch limousine, he just shook his head. He knew his father didn't understand. Kids had never been particularly kind to Jackson. It didn't help that he'd skipped kindergarten and the first grade, and was now the smallest kid in the eighth grade, or that his father was widely known as the second wealthiest man in Silicon Valley. So when Jackson had asked his father if he could attend the Blackfoot Braves Society Summer Camp nestled at the base of Granite Peak in Montana, he'd hoped to spend the entire summer without anyone knowing he was son of Clifford Brady, the president and CEO of Brady Technologies.

"Um ... excuse me," Jackson mumbled.

The chauffeur looked back at him in the rear-view mirror.

"Would you drop me off a mile or so away from the campground? I'll walk the rest of the way."

The chauffeur adjusted the mirror to get a better view of Jackson. "Come again?"

"I just don't want the other kids seeing me being dropped off in a limousine," he said.

"Really? Why not?"

Jackson shifted uneasily in the seat. "I don't want them thinking I'm rich or anything."

The chauffeur squinted his eyes, confused. He kept looking from the road into the rear-view mirror. "You're

Clifford Brady's kid, right?"

Jackson nodded his head.

"Kid, you are rich. Your dad is one of the richest men in the United States. What's the big deal? So you're rich. Who cares?"

"Other kids that aren't rich," Jackson said.

The limousine slowed down and turned off the interstate onto a gravel road, following a sign that read: B.B.S. – 3 miles.

The chauffeur looked back in the rear-view mirror. "Jackson, I'm sorry, but I was hired to pick you up from the airport and drop you off at the summer camp. I can't let you walk a mile to the camp. I'd get fired."

Jackson nodded his head and looked out the window at the passing blur of trees. "It's okay. I understand. I just thought I'd ask."

Jackson and the chauffeur drove in silence the rest of the way.

Children poured off three yellow buses as the limousine pulled to a stop under the weatherworn wooden sign that read: Blackfoot Braves Society Summer Camp. Jackson thought maybe he was imagining things, but he could've sworn the sound of laughter and playful banter quickly died as the chauffeur stepped out of the vehicle and opened the back door. He felt everyone's eyes on him as he timidly got out of the back of the limousine. The chauffeur saw Jackson carrying his suitcase and quickly snatched it out of his hands.

Jackson looked around the crowd of boys and girls staring at him with a combination of curiosity, jealousy, and contempt. He felt like his stomach was lodged in his throat. He was having a hard time catching his breath. He stood there for what seemed like an hour before the children forgot about him and the limousine and continued on their way.

"You must be Jackson Brady," a voice called out.

Jackson looked up and saw a man holding a clipboard and a pen made out of a bird's feather approaching him. The man extended his hand to Jackson, who shook it.

"I'm Bill Acebedo, but you can call me Chief Running Bear at Midnight for short," Bill said.

Jackson looked at Bill blankly. "Okay."

Bill tossed his head back and howled. "I'm just kiddin', Jackson. Call me Bill." He inspected the limousine with approving eyes as he grabbed the suitcase from the chauffeur. "Nice ride you got here, Jackson. You mind if I borrow it tonight–I want to trick my wife into believing I won the lottery. Are you cool with that?"

Jackson looked at the chauffeur who rolled his eyes. "I don't know…I think the driver was just supposed to drop me off. I don't know if my dad–"

Bill threw his head back as he howled with laughter again. "Jackson, I'm just kidding. You've got to relax. You're on vacation, so act like it and enjoy yourself."

"Okay. I'll try," Jackson said.

Bill rested his arm around Jackson's shoulder as he led him into the grounds. "Let me show you around the world famous Blackfoot Braves Society Summer Camp."

BLACKFOOT

CHAPTER TWO
Making Friends

Jackson struggled to keep up with Bill as he made his way into the heart of the summer camp. Kids ran in every direction, camp counselors frantically tried to keep the children organized in single-file lines, and a pack of dogs, tails wagging and barking, just added to the chaos.

"The first day of camp tends to be overwhelming," Bill said, "but it should settle down by this evening."

There was so much energy in the air that the hair on Jackson's neck stood up. Another counselor, who could barely carry all the bows and arrows in his arms, strolled up to Bill.

"Hey, Bill, where did you want these?" he asked.

"Jackson, this is Leon Mesa," Bill said. "Leon is your archery instructor. He'll have you shooting soda cans from a mile away before the summer is over."

Some of the arrows Leon held tumbled to the ground. Jackson bent down and pick them up, setting them gently on the tall pile in Leon's arms.

"Thanks, kid," Leon said.

"Leon, this is Jackson Brady," Bill said.

Leon's face lit up as he turned to look at Jackson. "No kiddin'? Your dad's Clifford–"

"Leon, you can stash those bows and arrows in my bunkhouse. Just set them on my bed," Bill said, cutting Leon off.

Leon looked from Jackson to Bill and back to Jackson before sauntering off.

"Let's keep moving along, Jackson," Bill smiled. "Lots to do."

A group of boys and girls carrying towels and wearing swimming suits almost ran over Bill and Jackson on their way to the river.

"Once we assign you to a tribe and you get settled into your bunk house," Bill said, "you can take a dip in the river too."

Jackson watched as a boy took hold of the large rope hanging on the bank of the river and swung over the water, only letting go as he arced high into the air. The boy splashed into the water.

"The river is fed from melted snow." Bill smiled, "So it's really cold. Just a warning."

The boy who splashed into the water reemerged with a startled shout and an expression that was a cross between pain and shock. He nearly jumped out of the water and onto the riverbank. Jackson could've sworn the boy's lips turned deep blue.

"The Blackfoot Braves Society Summer Camp was founded back in 1945 by Old Man Terry Timbisha," Bill said. "The story is he went on a hunting trip and got separated from his party after a thunderstorm rolled in. When he finally hiked out a few days later, he proclaimed that he was

buying this land and building a summer camp for boys and girls. Terry said it was to train warriors to ensure balance was restored to the world. I don't know about that, but his summer camp has hosted thousands and thousands of children since it opened way back when."

"What happened to Terry?" Jackson asked.

"Old Man Terry passed away back in 1973," Bill said. "I wasn't there, but I've heard while on his deathbed, his last words were, 'Find the three … they are the only ones who can bring balance to the world.'"

Bill stopped outside a bunkhouse and looked at the clipboard in his hand.

"What did he mean?" Jackson asked.

Shrugging his shoulders, Bill said, "Got me. Terry was a bit loco, if you know what I mean. Well, this is your new home for the next two months. What do you think?"

A smile spread across Jackson's mouth. "It's just how I imagined it would be."

The bunkhouse looked like a photo of the army barracks Jackson's uncle had slept in during basic training.

Bill opened the screen door, holding it open for Jackson. "Let's go meet the members of your tribe. They should all be getting settled in right about now."

The bunkhouse was one large room lined with two

rows of bunk beds, for a total of twenty beds. The bunkhouse bustled with activity as boys laid claim to the bunks they wanted.

Bill pulled a whistle, which hung on a string around his neck, out from underneath his shirt and blew it. The boys in the bunkhouse stopped in their tracks and turned their attention to Bill and Jackson, who shifted uneasily as all eyes focused on him.

"Boys, please let me have your attention for a moment," Bill said, loudly. "The Blackfoot Nation consists of four distinct Blackfoot tribes, which all have their own chiefs. These tribes are the Siksika, the Akainawa, the Pikanii, and the Blackfeet Nation. As you may already know, everyone assigned to this bunkhouse is the Blackfoot Nation. This is your designation for the rest of the summer. You will always know where you're supposed to be by reading the activities schedule posted outside the counselor's bunkhouse. Look for the Blackfoot listing at a particular time, and it will tell you where your tribe should be."

Jackson looked at the faces of the boys in the

bunkhouse, and he noticed not one of them was looking at Bill. Everyone silently judged Jackson with piercing eyes. He

couldn't hold their stares, so he looked up at Bill, but he could feel the glares.

"I want all of you to meet Jackson," Bill said, resting

his arm on his shoulder. "After you all get settled into your bunks, you as a tribe need to elect a chief, who's responsible for running the day-to-day operations of the tribe. I'm going to suggest you elect Jackson here."

Jackson couldn't believe his ears. He looked up at Bill, who winked down at him. Jackson looked around the bunkhouse at the boys staring back at him with contempt. He heard a couple of groans, but he didn't see who they came from.

"Anyway, I'm sure you boys will all become the best of friends over the course of the summer," Bill said, setting Jackson's suitcase down on the nearest bunk bed. "I'll let you all get acquainted."

Bill turned and walked out of the bunkhouse.

Jackson walked over to the bunk where his suitcase rested and was about to climb up onto the top bunk, when all of a sudden his suitcase came flying down off the bed. The suitcase hit Jackson in the chest and sent him tumbling to the ground with a thud.

The bunkhouse erupted with thunderous laughter.

All the boys pointed at Jackson lying on the floor with his suitcase pinning him. The wind had been forced out of Jackson's lungs, and he couldn't gather the strength to push it off his chest.

Before Jackson knew what was happening, someone lifted the suitcase off his chest and offered a hand to help him up. Jackson took the hand, and the other boy hoisted him to his feet.

"You okay, buddy?"

Jackson dusted himself off and looked at an Asian boy standing before him wearing baggy jeans, a bright white T-shirt, basketball shoes, and a baseball hat that sat slightly askew on his head.

"What was your name again?"

"Jackson Brady," he mumbled.

"I'm Austin Kim," the boy said. "Just to get it out of the way—no, I'm not Japanese or Chinese, I'm Korean-American."

"Um ... okay." Jackson stammered.

"Hey, what are you doing?!" a voice bellowed.

"Why'd you help that rich brat? That was funny!"

Jackson and Austin turned to look at a redheaded boy with freckles towering above them. In just a second's glance, Jackson knew the kind of boy the redhead was. He was a bully. Jackson had been dealing with his kind his entire life. It didn't matter where he went, Jackson always seemed to be surrounded by bullies sooner or later.

The redheaded boy poked a finger at Austin's chest. "Didn't you hear me? I asked why you pulled that suitcase off him."

Austin stared at the redhead boy with indifference.

"Don't you speak English?" the redhead boy sneered, taking a threatening step toward Austin.

"Guys, why don't we just calm down," Jackson said. "We haven't even—"

The redhead boy shoved at Jackson, but before he made contact, Austin reached out and grabbed the redheaded boy's hand, twisting it behind his back. The bigger boy snarled in pain as Austin twisted his hand up and forced him to his knees.

Bullies always seemed to find Jackson

"Yes, I do speak English," Austin said. "And I didn't catch your name."

Austin looked up just in time to see four friends of the redheaded boy rush toward him. He twisted the boy's hand even tighter, and the redhead boy winced in pain.

"Tell your friends to back off."

"Guys...stop...back off," the boy yelled.

"And I still haven't caught your name," Austin said again.

"Craig."

"Okay, Craig, let me break down how this is going to work," Austin said, cracking a smile. "I'm going to let you up, but only if you promise to go about your business. Do you understand?"

Craig nodded his head.

"Good."

Austin released his grip on Craig's hand and backed away toward Jackson. Craig jumped up, his face a mask of rage. He sized up Austin with fiery eyes. He must outweigh Austin by thirty pounds, Jackson thought. But surprisingly,

Craig thought better of it, and turned and walked over the top bunk where Jackson's suitcase had rested.

"Tell the rich brat to find another bunk," Craig barked. "This is mine."

Jackson picked his suitcase up off the floor and followed Austin to the back of the bunkhouse, past Craig's friends, who cleared a path for the boys to pass.

"You two better watch your backs," Craig said. "It's going to be a long summer."

Jackson followed Austin to his bunk.

"This is my bunk," Austin said. "You can put your stuff on the top one if you want."

"Thanks," Jackson said, as he tossed his suitcase on the bed over

Austin's. "And thanks for that back there."

Austin shrugged it off as he sat down on his bed. "No worries. That guy's been a major pain the whole bus ride here. It was my pleasure."

Jackson sat down next to Austin. "What was that back there? Do you know karate or something?"

"My grandfather taught me Tae Kwon Do way back when," Austin said.

"Wow, that's cool," Jackson said. "Are you a black belt?"

Austin laughed. "Nah...I just know enough to keep me out of trouble."

Austin and Jackson looked up and saw Craig and his friends whispering and shooting glares their way.

"I hope you know enough to keep yourself out of trouble with our new friends," Jackson said.

"Tell you what, you watch my back this summer and I'll watch yours," Austin said. "Between the two of us, we should be able to get by."

Craig, cracking his knuckles, looked Jackson

in the eyes.

"We might need to recruit more help, Austin," Jackson choked.

"My summer vacation is starting out on the wrong foot, that's for sure," Austin laughed.

CHAPTER THREE
From Bad to Worse

Jackson and Austin sat next to each other at a table in the dining hall. Each of the four tables was assigned to one of the tribes at the summer camp–the Siksika, Akainawa, Pikanii, and the Blackfeet Nation, which was the table where Jackson and Austin sat.

The noise in the dining hall was nearly deafening as the kids ate their dinner. In just a few hours, rivalries had already developed between the tribes. Jackson had witnessed the members of his tribe rally behind the newly elected chief–Craig.

After finding out he was the chief, the redheaded boy had pointed his finger like a gun at Jackson and Austin and pretended to pull the trigger.

"You could see that coming a mile away," Austin whispered in Jackson's ear. "Just our luck."

Jackson was trying hard to remember why he wanted to come to this summer camp so badly, but he just couldn't think of a reason right now. So far, things hadn't gone how he'd envisioned. His whole life Jackson had been treated one of two ways—either people were overly polite and nice to him to get in good with his father, or they were mean to him because he was the son of a wealthy man. As far as he was concerned, Jackson just wished people would treat him like everyone else.

"So, how is everything going?"

Jackson and Austin looked up at Bill.

"I heard you boys had a little trouble after I left the bunkhouse this afternoon," Bill said. "What happened?"

Jackson and Austin looked at each other for a moment before Austin turned to Bill and asked, "Really? What did you hear?"

"I heard you got into a little tussle with Craig."

Jackson glanced over at Craig, who was glaring at him from across the table. Craig mouthed 'Keep your mouth shut' to Jackson, but Bill looked over at Craig at that moment.

"What did you say, chief? You're going to have to speak up."

Craig, knowing he was busted, tried to look anywhere but at Bill, who stormed around the table and stood over Craig.

"Craig, you're the chief of your tribe," Bill said, frowning. "You need to act like it. Why don't you go back to your bunk and think about how you're going act like a leader?"

Craig got up with a huff. As he walked past Jackson and Austin, he hissed, "I'm gonna get you two for this."

Jackson watched Craig storm outside. "He looks mad."

"That guy's ornerier than a rattlesnake," Austin said,

as he dug into his dinner.

Jackson looked at his food and realized he'd lost his appetite. He pushed his plate away.

"You're not going to finish your dinner?" Austin asked.

Jackson shook his head no.

"Can I have your fry bread?"

"Sure."

Austin scooped up the fry bread and tore into it with relish. "Man, this stuff is tasty. I could live just on it alone."

Jackson scanned the dining hall, looking at all the other boys and girls laughing, smiling, and joking as they ate dinner with their tribes. He envied how other kids his age seemed like they didn't have a single care in the world. Jackson couldn't remember a time when he felt carefree. Maybe he did before his mother died, Jackson thought, but he couldn't remember much from back then.

His entire life Jackson felt like he carried a weight on his shoulders that he couldn't explain. Except for not having any true friends, Jackson had a pretty good life; he got straight As in school, was the captain of the debate club and the math club, and was the under 18 state chess champion. Even with all that, Jackson couldn't shake the feeling that he somehow wasn't living up to his potential. He couldn't put his finger on it, but no matter what he did or accomplished, he just couldn't escape it.

As Jackson drank the last of his water, he felt a set of eyes staring at him. He glanced over and spotted a girl sitting at another table being virtually ignored by all the other kids around her. The girl tore a piece of fry bread off her plate and stuck it in the pocket on the front of her sweatshirt, the whole time holding Jackson's stare. He watched as the girl pinched off another piece of her fry bread and stuffed it in her pocket. But this time Jackson caught a glimpse of a small animal poking its head out. It devoured the fry bread, then disappeared back inside the girl's sweatshirt. Jackson, startled, looked back at the girl, who was smiling at him. She quickly picked her tray up and walked off.

"Who is that girl?" Jackson asked.

"Which girl?" Austin said.

Jackson pointed at the girl in the sweatshirt as she scraped her plate into the garbage, tossed her dirty utensils onto a pile, and stacked her tray on a rack.

"Oh, that's Mazzy," Austin said, picking more food off Jackson's plate. "She was here last summer, and she just hung out by herself in the forest."

"What did she do in the forest?"

"How should I know?" Austin said. "Why do you care?"

Jackson shrugged his shoulders as he watched Mazzy walk out of the dining hall by herself.

The three warriors were enslaved by the Great Serpent

CHAPTER FOUR
History Lesson

The next few days were a blur for Jackson. The camp schedule was packed full of activities like fishing, basket making, survival training, and bow and arrow practice. But Jackson's favorite was learning about the history of the Blackfoot Indians.

He found out that thousands of years ago, the Blackfoot Indians were nomadic buffalo hunters that migrated to the Great Plains area, which included present-day Montana. The nomadic Blackfoot Indians were known for their great skills in hunting the enormous buffalo long before the first pyramids of Egypt were built. The term

"Blackfoot" came from the tribe's habit of dyeing their moccasins black.

Until 1730, when the Blackfoot first acquired horses, the tribe traveled on foot. Soon after, the tribe became renowned for their expert horsemanship. They had a reputation as fierce warriors, and by the mid-19th century controlled a vast amount of territory stretching from northern Saskatchewan to the southernmost waters of the Missouri. They were also known as the strongest Indian tribe in the northwestern plains, but by the end of the century, their population was decimated. In the winter of 1884, the buffalo were nearly extinct and many Blackfoot Indians starved.

Jackson's favorite story was about four Blackfoot warriors that set out from their tribe's camp during the winter of 1884 to venture to the top of the Granite Mountain to perform the Sun Dance. The Sun Dance was a ritual that was believed to renew prosperity and social harmony for the coming year. The four warriors hoped to receive supernatural aid from Mother Earth, who would bestow power through the warriors' sacrifice. The warriors would use this power to help provide for their tribe, which was on the verge of death.

Ma–Tas–Kah, the strongest of the war- riors, led the other three to the top of Granite Mountain. There the four men danced for days on end while fasting and abstaining

from drink. They used skewers to pierce their skin and muscles as part of the self-torture–this self-inflicted pain reflected the warriors' desire to return something of themselves to nature in exchange for future benefits.

The Sun Dance went on for weeks and weeks, until all four warriors collapsed in exhaustion, weak from not eating or drinking and from loss of blood. In this weakened state, Mother Earth looked into the heart of Ma–Tas–Kah and saw he was the wisest of the warriors and appeared to him.

Mother Earth gave him his animal spirit totem, which was the owl. The warrior was told his animal spirit totem would give him great powers. Mother Earth told Ma–Tas–Kah that the circle of harmony on Earth had been broken, and this was why his people, along with others across the planet, were dying needlessly. To restore balance, Mother Earth gave him three other animal spirit totems, the bison, the wolf, and the raven, and it was his responsibility to find three worthy warriors to pass these animal totems and their powers onto them. Then, and only then, would they be able to stop the coming storm Mother Earth saw on the horizon, restoring the circle of harmony.

When Ma–Tas–Kah awoke, Mother Earth had vanished. He told his three friends of his vision, who told him to give them the sacred animal spirit totems. But Ma–Tas–Kah said he didn't know if his three friends were the worthy warriors Mother Earth had told him to find. The three warriors grew angry with Ma–Tas–Kah, and they cursed him and Mother Earth.

The three warriors invoked the spirit of the Great

Serpent, and asked for the power that had been denied to them by Ma–Tas–Kah. This ancient evil appeared as a serpent-like wind funnel and circled around the three warriors before disappearing inside them, taking over their souls and filling their eyes with its black light. The Great Serpent used the three warriors' bodies as its vessel, bending their will to its own. They were no longer men–they were Sta–au, evil spirits capable of inhabiting and controlling everything, from animals to deceased ancestors to wind and rain. These three Sta–au were enslaved by the Great Serpent.

Ma–Tas–Kah and the three Sta–au clashed in battle on the top of Granite Mountain. This fight waged for years, and with each passing year, they fell further and further into the great mountain. At the end, Ma–Tas–Kah vanquished the Sta–au far beneath Granite Mountain. Ma–Tas–Kah was never seen again, and tribal legend claims that he was so weak from the battle that he had to remain in the mountain.

The legend told that the howling winds are actually Ma–Tas–Kah wailing as he slumbers under Granite Mountain. His spirit will only be free when he finds three warriors to bestow the sacred animal totems, restoring the circle of balance.

After hearing Bill share this legend, Jackson found himself thinking about the story that night as he got ready for bed.

"What do you think about that legend of the Sta–au?" Jackson asked. "If it's true, they're being held captive near this camp under the mountain."

Austin spit toothpaste

into the sink and wiped his mouth.

"Dude, it's just a story," Austin said. "A crazy story to boot."

"I don't think it's crazy at all," Jackson said, flossing his teeth in the mirror. "I like the idea of three warriors coming along and restoring balance in the world."

"Yeah, but the bigger concern would be the three Sta–au trapped underneath Granite Mountain that would come along with that balance."

"What do you mean?"

Austin put his toothbrush in his toiletry bag and zipped it up. "Come on, Jackson. Do you actually believe the Sta–au are just going to allow the three warriors to 'restore balance' in the world without having a say in the matter?"

Jackson and Austin climbed into their bunk beds. Jackson leaned over the side of his bed and looked down at Austin.

"But they're trapped underneath the mountain,"

Jackson said. "What can they do about it?"

"Yeah...trapped, not buried, trapped," Austin said, fluffing his pillow. "If Ma–Tas–Kah had to sleep for years and years to regain his strength, maybe the Sta–au are just sleeping to regain theirs. Anyways, it's just a legend. Nobody believes this stuff. Go to sleep."

Jackson rested his head on his pillow and thought, "Yeah, it's just a legend."

He drifted off to sleep to the sound of thunder cracking in the distance.

CHAPTER FIVE
The Burial

Jackson lay on his bunk bed after lunch reading a book when Bill popped his head in the bunkhouse door.

"Jackson, your father's on the phone," he said.

Jackson looked up from his book.

"You can use the phone in my office."

Jackson jumped up and followed Bill into his office. Stuffed animal heads were mounted on the walls. The room smelled like a thrift store Jackson had visited once back home—musty and stuffy. Jackson looked around at the buffalo, deer, and elk heads before picking up the phone.

"Hello," Jackson said.

"Jackson, it's your father," Clifford said. "How are you doing?"

"Everything's going great, Dad."

"Your counselor, Bill, told me you had a problem with some of the other boys in camp. Is that true?"

Jackson rolled his eyes. "It wasn't a big deal, Dad. Just a misunderstanding."

The phone went silent for a moment, and Jackson knew his father was taking it all in. He heard a deep breath and exhale before his father said, "If you want to come home, I'll send the plane to pick you up. I don't want you to feel like you have to stay there on my account."

"Dad, I'm the one who had to

talk you in to letting me come here for the summer," Jackson said. "I'm doing fine. Don't worry."

"Okay, son," Clifford said. "I just wanted to check in on you and make sure you're all right."

"Doing great."

"Well, call me if you need anything."

"Okay, Dad," Jackson said.

"Love you, son."

"I love you, too, Dad."

Jackson heard his father hang up the phone, and Jackson did the same. He looked up and saw Bill standing outside the screen door looking in.

"Everything okay?" Bill asked.

Jackson walked outside onto the porch next to Bill. He saw Mazzy walking by herself into the forest, holding a small shovel. Jackson couldn't be sure, but he thought he saw an animal resting on her shoulder as she disappeared in the woods. "Um, yeah … everything's fine," he said, distracted.

"That's good. I had a little talk with your father before I came and got you," Bill said. "I hope you don't mind. Sometimes summer camp is harder on parents than it is on their kids."

Jackson squinted as he tried to see Mazzy, but she was gone. Bill looked at his wristwatch. "It looks like you have a little time to kill before your tribe's next class, so you can go back to reading your book if you want."

Jackson hopped off the porch and ran into the forest in the direction Mazzy had disappeared. "Okay ... thanks," he yelled back at Bill.

Jackson stopped on the edge of the forest and tried to spot Mazzy, but the tall trees blocked out the sunshine, making it hard to see more than a few feet. Jackson pushed aside tree branches and stepped into the woods.

He had to protect his face from the evergreen needles, but it didn't take too long before he reached a clearing. There he saw Mazzy, looking like she was digging a hole. Jackson approached her slowly.

"Hey," Jackson called out.

Mazzy looked up. "Hello," she said, looking back down at her feet.

Jackson walked up and saw what she was doing. Mazzy was digging a hole to bury dead animals.

"What happened to them?" Jackson asked.

"I don't know," Mazzy said. "But it's not good."

Jackson took a closer look at the dead animals, which were a badger, porcupine, and a bobcat, and he saw the carcasses had patches of raw and bloody exposed skin all over their bodies, like their fur and quills had been scratched off.

"At first I would just find one here and there, and they were smaller animals," Mazzy said, "but now I always find three dead animals lying next to each other almost every single day, and they're getting bigger."

Mazzy continued digging. The hole was pretty big, and she looked like she was tired.

"Do you need a hand?" Jackson asked.

Mazzy stopped digging and handed the shovel to him. "Thanks. I'm beat."

While Jackson dug, he saw Mazzy feed bits of bread to a chipmunk in the pocket on her sweatshirt.

"That's cool," Jackson said. "Is it your pet?"

"I don't know if you could call him a pet," Mazzy smiled. "I think he's just using me for free meals and easy transportation."

"I didn't know you could tame a chipmunk."

"Oh, you can tame just about any animal," Mazzy said. "It just takes time and patience, but I don't recommend doing it with an animal that can maul you."

They worked together to place the animal carcasses in the grave and cover them.

"I'll keep that in mind," Jackson said, as he finished packing dirt over the mound. "Okay, all done."

Jackson handed the shovel back to Mazzy as they headed back to camp. Right as they stepped out of the forest, a slight breeze rustled the tree branches. Jackson stopped in his tracks and whirled around. He felt all the blood drain from his face, and he felt lightheaded.

"What's wrong?" Mazzy asked.

"I don't know," he said. "I...felt something ...bad."

"Bad? Like what?"

"Like evil just reached out and tapped me on the shoulder," Jackson said.

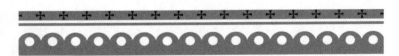

CHAPTER SIX
Take a Hike

The next day, every tribe at the Blackfoot Braves Society Summer Camp was going to participate in a joint activity that involved a three-day outing to the top of Granite Mountain. It would take a full day to hike to the top of the mountain, a day to explore the area, and a day's travel back to camp.

Jackson had been looking forward to it ever since hearing the story of Ma–Tas–Kah battling the Sta–au on top of the legendary mountain. He wanted to see where this epic battle supposedly took place.

The day of the hike, Jackson packed his backpack and prepared for the day's excursion. Austin lay on his bed reading a comic book. He looked at Jackson with mild amusement.

"I don't know what you're so excited about," Austin said. "It's a four-hour hike to the top of the mountain, and for what? To look down and see the summer camp. Big whoop."

Jackson stuffed his canteen into his pack. "Aren't you just a little curious to see where the epic battle of all time occurred?" Jackson asked. "It's a part of history."

"Since when are legends history?" Austin laughed. "Since never, that's when."

Jackson stopped packing and looked down at Austin. "Just because you don't understand something or can't explain it doesn't mean it doesn't exist. Let your mind embrace other possibilities…suspend disbelief and let your imagination run wild. Isn't that the gift of being our age?"

Austin smiled and shook his head at Jackson. "Whatever you say, Jackson. Whatever you say."

Bill came into the bunkhouse holding a clipboard. "Is everyone ready for the hike?"

Everyone shouted they were ready.

Craig pushed his way through the crowd and stood

next to Bill.

"Before we head out, I have a couple of announcements as your chief," Craig said. "I forgot to mention this before, but I regret to announce that the counselors have decided that two members of the Blackfoot Nation will have to stay behind at camp with Bill just in case any emergencies arise."

Austin got up off his bed and put a hand on Jackson's shoulder. "Oh, boy. I'll bet I know who's not going."

Craig lifted his hand pointed toward Jackson and Austin. "As your chief, I decided that Jackson and Austin will be the most capable to deal with any events that may arise while the rest of the camp is gone for the next three days."

"What? Are you kidding?" Jackson said. "I want to go on the hike."

"Silence!" Craig hollered. "Your chief has spoken!

Now, the rest of the Blackfoot Nation, let's head out!"

Jackson watched as everyone in the bunkhouse picked up their backpacks and followed Craig toward Granite Mountain.

Jackson threw his pack to the ground with a force that surprised Austin. "That's not fair!" he yelled. "Craig must've known I was looking forward to going on this trip."

"He's a class-A jerk," Austin said. "But just think about it, we'll be here in camp by ourselves for three days. That's going to be cool. We can do what we want when we want."

"I don't know if that's necessarily true."

Jackson and Austin look up and saw Bill grinning at them.

"Remember, boys, I'm going to be here in camp, too," Bill said. "I'm not going to let you run around setting fire to the place or anything."

"Oh, come, on, Bill," Austin joked. "We wouldn't do something like that. We'd just torch Craig's bed."

"I'm sorry about you not being able to go, guys," Bill said. "Every year there are a couple of kids that have to stay behind, and the counselors randomly pick the tribe whose chief will decide who the unlucky ones will be. This year it was your tribe."

"We're just going to hang around here and watch the campground?" asked an irritated Jackson. "So I had to talk my father into letting me come to this summer camp to be a de facto security guard?"

"I'm sure I'll be able to find something fun for you guys to do." Bill smiled.

Bill turned to walk out of the bunkhouse. "Why don't you guys go into the mess hall and make yourself some lunch? Whatever you want."

Jackson and Austin walked into the empty mess hall and made their way back to the kitchen.

"Dude, I'm going to eat hot dogs for the next three days," Austin said. "No way am I eating those crummy green beans they try to feed us here. I'll race you for the marshmallows."

Austin sprinted off, leaving Jackson sulking in his wake. The other boy disappeared inside the large pantry in the kitchen, but right when Jackson saw him turn on the light, he heard a bloodcurdling scream.

Jackson ran into the pantry and found Austin lying on the floor. Mazzy stood above him, cradling her chipmunk to her chest.

"What happened?" Jackson asked.

Austin pointed at Mazzy and said, "She scared the daylights outta me!"

"You scared me!" Mazzy screamed. "You nearly trampled Hoover."

"What the heck were you doing hiding back here?" Austin yelled.

The chipmunk scurried inside Mazzy's sweatshirt.

"They told me I couldn't take Hoover with me on the trip to Granite Mountain, so I decide to just hide until everyone left," she said. "Come to think of it, what are you guys doing here?"

"We got picked to stay behind and hold down the fort," Austin said.

"Are we the only people left in camp?" she asked.

"Just us and Bill," Jackson said.

Austin got up off the floor and began rooting through the containers of food. "Man, it looks like we're going to have to cook this stuff."

Mazzy opened the large refrigerator door, revealing shelves of prepared food. Mazzy reached in and pulled out a foot-long hotdog. "Why don't you just eat these leftovers?"

Austin looked over at Mazzy as she bit into the hotdog.

"That's what I'm talkin' 'bout," Austin grinned. "Hand me one of those dogs."

Jackson, Austin, and Mazzy sat in the empty mess

hall and watched Hoover do tricks for food. For the first time since coming to camp, Jackson felt at ease. He hadn't realized until now, but his guard had been up ever since he'd arrived. Now, he was with two other kids who allowed him to just be himself. It was very comfortable, and Jackson couldn't remember the last time he could say that.

"What do we have here … a stowaway?"

The three kids turned to see Bill standing in the doorway of the mess hall. Jackson and Austin looked at Mazzy as she did her best to scoop up Hoover and try to conceal the chipmunk.

"Aren't you supposed to be with your tribe, Mazzy?" Bill asked.

"I couldn't go with them."

"Why not?"

Mazzy looked at Jackson and Austin for help, but the boys shrugged their shoulders. Bill walked over to the kids and spotted Hoover's head pop up and sniff the air.

"When I first came to the Blackfoot Braves Society Summer Camp way back when," Bill said, "I caught a baby squirrel. I wanted to tame it, but one of the other kids from my tribe pulled a mean trick and let it go."

Bill reached down with his finger and let Hoover sniff it.

"Be careful that one of the girls from your tribe doesn't do the same thing," Bill said.

"You're not going to make me let him go?" Mazzy asked. "I just knew if anyone found out about him they'd make me get rid of him."

"Is that why you didn't go on the hike to Granite Mountain ... because of your new pet?"

"Yeah."

Bill scratched his chin. "I guess I'll have to call the rest of the counselors on the walkie-talkie and let them know you're here in camp so they don't worry about you. I'll tell them you fell asleep under a tree and missed going with them. How's that?"

"Thanks."

"Well, it's not going to be all fun and games while the rest of the camp is gone," Bill said. "I've got a mission for you three. I'll tell you tonight at dinner."

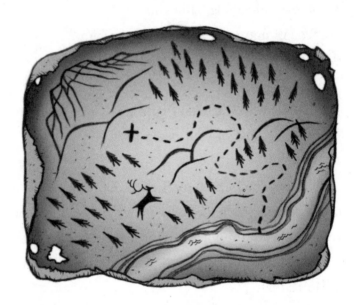

CHAPTER SEVEN
Hidden Treasure

That night, sitting around a campfire roasting hotdogs, Bill pulled out a map and held it up. "Almost twenty years ago, a counselor here at camp gave me this map. He said it would lead me to a hidden treasure," Bill said.

"Hidden treasure? You're kiddin'," Austin laughed.

"Supposedly, the Blackfoot tribe buried a cache of riches as European settlers encroached on their territory centuries ago."

Jackson pulled his hotdog, which was on a long stick, out of the fire and put it on a bun. "Did you find anything?"

"Nah," Bill said. "I searched the whole area for a full

Hidden treasure just waiting to be found

day, but we didn't find anything."

"Can I see the map?" Mazzy asked.

Bill handed the map over to Mazzy. She spread it on the ground. The fires cast eerie shadows across it. Jackson scooted over so he could look at it.

"I would've been mad if my counselor sent me on a wild goose chase," Austin said.

"Well, I guess you're going to be mad at me then," Bill laughed, squirting mustard onto his hotdog. "Because you three are heading into the hills to see if you have better luck than my friends and I had when we went looking for the treasure."

Mazzy and Jackson looked up from the map at Bill, both wearing smiles from ear-to-ear.

"Really?" Jackson asked.

"Are you serious?" Mazzy smiled.

"You betcha," Bill said, taking a big bite out of his hotdog. "I'll help you pack a lunch first thing in the morning, then you'll head off to find great riches."

"Man, I don't have any hiking shoes," Austin said,

pointing to his white basketball shoes. "My shoes will get dirty."

"Well, Austin, I guess you'd better find the buried treasure so you can buy yourself a new pair of shoes," Bill laughed. "Just think of it as a practical exercise on how to read a map."

"Oh, man," Austin moaned. "I'm allergic to hiking."

"Come on, Austin," Jackson said. "It'll be fun."

"You don't have to go if you don't want to, Austin," Bill said. "You can stay behind and help me dig the big fire pit for Friday's bonfire celebration when everyone gets back from Granite Mountain."

"Digging a hole?" Austin grimaced as he peered over at the map. "Man, I can barely read that thing. We might get lost and be attacked by wild animals or something."

"I'll give you a whistle you can blow if you suddenly get attacked by a chipmunk," Bill said. Right then, Hoover popped its head out of Mazzy's sweatshirt. "Sorry, I didn't mean any offense."

Jackson rested his hands on Austin's and Mazzy's

shoulders. "What time do you both want to leave tomorrow?"

The three kids all looked at the sun-faded map together. Jackson ran his finger along the dotted line that led from the river to the "X" that, hopefully, marked the spot of the buried treasure. Jackson's stomach was tied in knots from the anticipation of going on a treasure hunt. This was even better than hiking to the top of Granite Mountain.

As they sat around the campfire, a slight breeze kicked up just beyond the tree line surrounding the clearing. Jackson turned around and, for a second, could have sworn he saw three sets of eyes glowing from the edge of the forest. He blinked and the eyes were gone. A shiver ran down his spine as the wind kicked up, stirring the tree branches for a moment before dying down.

Jackson told himself he was imagining things as he turned his attention back to the adventure at hand.

CHAPTER EIGHT
The Cave

Before the sun rose the next day, Jackson, Austin, and Mazzy, all wearing backpacks and carrying small shovels, headed off in search of the treasure. Bill had helped them pack lunch, and he'd told them he'd have dinner ready when they got back that evening. He had wished the three kids luck and told them to be careful.

After a few hours on the trail, the sun was still climbing into the sky. It was already a hot day, and they decided to stop and rest in the shade of a tree for a little bit. Jackson pulled the map out from his backpack and unfolded it on the ground.

"I'm guessing it'll take us another hour or so before we get to the spot," he said.

"This is such a waste of time," Austin grumbled. "We should just stay here and head back in a few hours. We'll just tell Bill we searched for the treasure but couldn't find anything."

Mazzy took a drink of water from her canteen and then poured a little in her hand and let Hoover lap it up.

"Bill doesn't expect us to discover some treasure, Austin. It's just an excuse for us to explore the area and get out of camp for awhile."

Austin poured water from his canteen onto a handkerchief and attempted to rub dirt off his white basketball shoes. He dismissed Mazzy with a wave of the hand.

Jackson folded the map and stuffed it back into his pack. He used his hand to cover his eyes from the sun as he looked off toward the horizon. A patch of dark clouds seemed to be creeping their way.

"That doesn't look so good," Jackson said. "We better keep our eyes on that storm front."

Austin and Mazzy looked where Jackson pointed.

"We don't want to get caught out here in a storm," Jackson commented.

Jackson and Mazzy got up and headed down the trail. Austin hurried and tried to finish washing his shoes, but he finally gave up and stuffed the handkerchief into his pocket as he rushed to catch up with his friends.

Two hours later, Austin and Mazzy looked over Jackson's shoulder as he held the map. What had started out as a sunny day had turned into overcast one. They all knew they were lost, but none of them wanted to be the first to state the obvious.

"I don't know, guys," Jackson muttered. "Anyone

have any ideas?"

Austin looked up at the darkening sky. "I think we need to be getting back to camp. It's not looking so good out here."

Suddenly, the kids saw a bolt of lightning rip through the sky, followed closely by a booming clap of thunder.

"Let's keep moving," Mazzy said. "We've got to get out of here."

About ten minutes later, the sky opened up and began pouring torrents of rain. Jackson didn't know it was possible for it to rain that hard. He could barely see a foot in front of him as he tried to follow the trail, which he hoped led back to camp. He couldn't be sure were he was going. Jackson had never been this scared in his life. He wanted to stop and curl up underneath a tree and wait for someone to tell him what to do next. But Jackson felt Mazzy's hand on his shoulder, and he knew Austin's was on hers, so he kept moving because his friends were counting on him.

The storm must have been directly over them, because the bolts of lightning and the sound of thunder

happened at the exact same instant. Jackson knew they had to find shelter and fast. But where? he wondered. And almost as soon as he thought it, he spotted something at the base of the mountain. He sped up as he made his way toward it.

He didn't know how he'd seen anything in this storm, but just ahead was the mouth of a cave. A wave of relief washed over Jackson as he stepped out of the storm into the dry cave. Austin and Mazzy looked around in shock.

"How'd you find this?' Mazzy asked.

"I don't know," Jackson said. "I saw something and just made my way toward it."

"In this storm?" Austin asked. "I had to shut my eyes, it was raining so hard."

"Me too," Mazzy said.

Jackson looked around the cave too. It wasn't that big, maybe six feet tall and four feet wide. Jackson couldn't tell how far the cave went into the mountain because it was pitch black after only a few yards.

"How far back do you think this cave goes?" Austin asked.

"I have no idea," Jackson said. "But we'll just stay at the mouth until the storm passes."

Mazzy sat down, opened her pack, and pulled out her lunch. "I'm starving."

Jackson and Austin joined her, pulling their lunches out of their packs. They wolfed down the sandwiches Bill had packed for them.

"Does anyone know where we are?" Austin asked.

Mazzy and Jackson lowered their eyes, answering his question without saying a word.

"How are we going to find our way back?" he said.

"We'll worry about that once it stops raining," Jackson said.

Mazzy pinched off a piece of bread and feed it to a wet Hoover, who didn't seem to mind the predicament they were in.

Jackson finished eating his lunch and yawned. He was so tired. He couldn't remember being this tired. He laid his head down on his backpack and shut his eyes, falling asleep almost instantly.

CHAPTER NINE
Ma–Tas–Kah

Jackson awoke to Austin shaking him. He didn't know how long he'd been sleeping, but he looked outside the cave and saw that it was still raining pretty hard.

"Jackson, get up," Austin whispered. "There's something in this cave."

Austin pointed toward the back of the cave. Jackson looked in that direction, and couldn't believe what he saw. What looked like a green light appeared to be glowing further down in the cave's corridor.

"What is that?" Jackson asked.

"We have no idea," Austin said.

The light seemed to pulsate, growing dim, then bright, and then dim again. Jackson got up and took a couple of steps deeper into the cave.

"Jackson, what are you doing?" Mazzy asked.

"I'm going to see where that light is coming from," he said.

"Do you think that's a good idea?" Austin asked. "I mean, why don't we just get out of here?"

Jackson pointed at the rain and lightning that stormed just outside of the cave. "We'll never find our way back to camp in this weather."

Jackson picked up his pack and slung it on his back before heading off to see where the light was coming from.

Austin watched as Mazzy followed after Jackson. "Don't tell me you're going with him?"

"We should all stick together," Mazzy said.

"Yeah, let's stick together at the mouth of the cave," Austin said.

Mazzy shrugged her shoulders and continued

after Jackson.

Austin kicked a rock that lay at his feet. "I should've just gone to Disneyland with my parents this summer. But no, I had to come to the Blackfoot Braves Society Summer Camp. What was I thinking?"

Austin picked up his pack and chased after his friends.

It's strange, Jackson thought, the green light doesn't illuminate the corridor. If he took his eyes off the light, he was submerged in complete darkness. He couldn't tell where he was walking. Jackson just focused on walking toward the green light.

"Jackson, can you see where you're walking?" Mazzy asked. "Because I can't see where I'm going."

"If I take my eyes off the light," Jackson said, "I can't see anything."

Jackson felt Mazzy's hand rest on his shoulder. "Okay, well, I guess this really is the blind leading the blind."

"Don't forget about me," Austin shouted, echoing through the cave, making Jackson and Mazzy both jump in surprise.

"Austin, put your hand on my shoulder," Mazzy said.

Austin ran into the back of Mazzy. "Sorry. I didn't see you," he said.

The three friends headed off toward the unknown in a single-file line.

They walked toward the light for what seemed like forever, but they didn't seem to be getting any closer to discovering the source. Jackson turned around to look at the mouth of the cave, but all he saw behind him was utter darkness. Jackson had a hard time swallowing. He didn't know if they'd be able to find their way back. He kept moving toward the green light. Jackson knew their only hope was to move forward. He didn't know how he knew this, but he just did.

Right when Jackson was about ready to suggest they take a break, he stepped into a large cavern. The walls emitted the soft, green light. Jackson turned and could actually see Mazzy and Austin, who both looked around the cavern in awe.

"What is this place?" Mazzy asked.

"I don't know," Jackson said. "What do you think makes it glow like that?"

"It's the light of truth."

Jackson and Mazzy, both puzzled, looked at Austin.

"Huh?" Jackson asked.

"What?" Austin said.

"What do you mean 'it's the light of truth'?" Mazzy asked.

"Guys, I didn't say that," Austin said.

"If you didn't say it, who did?"

Suddenly, Jackson felt a powerful presence in the cave. He turned and saw a figure sitting crossed-legged on an altar made of stone. Behind the altar, a radiant waterfall cascaded down from the top of the cavern.

"I said it, my young ones," the figure said.

Austin nearly fell over when the saw the figure sitting there. Before Mazzy could stop Hoover, the chipmunk climbed out of her pocket and jumped to the cavern floor, racing over to the figure sitting on the altar.

"Hoover, come back," Mazzy pleaded.

The three kids watched as the chipmunk scurried up the platform and climbed onto the figure's lap. The man leaned down, revealing an old, Native American man with wrinkled skin and eyes that were completely white. His long, grey hair fell down past his shoulders. He wore a ceremonial gown that Blackfoot chiefs wore in pictures in books Jackson had read while at camp.

"Well, hello, little one," the man said as he picked up Hoover and scratched the chipmunk behind its ear.

The old man looked at the three children standing before him. "Come forward so I might see you better."

Jackson didn't hesitate before walking toward the altar the man sat upon. Mazzy and Austin followed.

"We have much to discuss and not much time," the

old man said.

Jackson, Mazzy, and Austin stood before the old man. He looked them over, studying them, before nodding his head with approval. "I've waited a very long time for you three to come here."

The three children looked at each other, then back at

the old man. They couldn't believe their ears.

"I think you've got the wrong people," Austin said.

The old man smiled as he peered into Austin's eyes. "You're the three warriors I've been waiting for."

Jackson felt like he'd been hit in the stomach. He felt light-headed, and he realized he'd forgotten to breathe.

"Ma–Tas–Kah?" Jackson whispered.

The old man turned to Jackson. "Yes, boy, I am Ma–Tas–Kah."

"It can't be." Austin shook his head. "It was all just a legend, right?"

The old man threw his head back and laughed with a roar that shook the walls of the   cavern.

"I'm just a legend?" Ma–Tas–Kah howled. "I've often wished that I was, son. Because if I were, then that would mean that the Sta–au would also just be lore."

"This can't be happening," Jackson mumbled.

"What are you two talking about?" Mazzy asked.

"This is Ma–Tas–Kah," Jackson said. "He battled

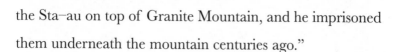

the Sta–au on top of Granite Mountain, and he imprisoned them underneath the mountain centuries ago."

The old man leaned toward Jackson and said, "But they've escaped, and it's going to be your job to vanquish them once and for all."

The three warriors are given their spirit totems

CHAPTER TEN
The Great Serpent

Jackson couldn't believe his ears, and he could tell from their expressions that neither could Austin or Mazzy. It was then that he realized they weren't actually hearing Ma–Tas–Kah with their ears, but in their minds. Jackson looked closer at the man on the altar and saw that the words he spoke were in his native language, which he and his friends wouldn't be able to understand.

"The Sta–au are skin-shifters," the old man said. "Their evil spirits travel across the land in a wind that comes to rest in the bodies of their prey. They drain the life force of the creatures and leave them for dead once their evil spirits exit. So far, the Sta–au have only had the strength to inhabit small creatures. But as their power grows, so does their ability to possess bigger animals. The Sta–au don't feel comfortable in the bodies they steal, and they scratch themselves constantly, sometimes taking off chunks of flesh."

Mazzy turned to Jackson. "Remember the animals in the forest?"

"Yeah, they were probably inhabited by the Sta–au," he said, turning his attention back to Ma–Tas–Kah. "Can they jump into the bodies of humans?"

"Yes, soon they'll be able to possess the bodies of men and women," the old man said.

"What do the Sta–au want?" Mazzy asked.

"The Sta–au were once my tribesmen, and they were warped into the evil they are by the Great Serpent," Ma–Tas–Kah said. "The Great Serpent is the sum total of all the resentments of mankind, so when the Sta–au were spawned, they had only one desire—revenge on mankind for their existence."

"This can't be happening," Jackson muttered, shaking his head in disbelief. He'd heard some fantastic things in his life, but this just too much to handle. His brain couldn't begin to make sense of what he was hearing.

"I have waited for hundreds of years for three warriors to make themselves known to me so I could bestow them with their spirit totems. Then and only then would they be capable of defeating the Sta–au and the Great Serpent that spawned them, which will restore the circle of harmony to the world," Ma–Tas–Kah said.

The old man smiled and motioned for Austin to come to him. Austin looked nervously at Jackson for an indication of what he should do. Jackson shrugged his shoulders.

"Do not fear, Austin," Ma–Tas–Kah said. "I mean you no harm."

Austin stepped toward the old man. "How do you know my name?"

The old man rested a weary hand on Austin's shoulder. "I know everything about you, boy. I know that you are a mischievous young man, but you have a good heart who'd never cause anyone any harm."

Jackson watched in awe as he saw the old man's hand begin to glow.

"Your spirit totem will be the wolf," Ma–Tas–Kah said, laying his glowing hand on Austin's head. "Mischievous, playful, but fast as the wind."

With a stunned look on his face, Austin stumbled back and collapsed to the ground. Jackson raced to him. It looked like he had fallen into a deep sleep. Jackson tried to wake him, but no matter what he did, Austin remained soundly asleep.

"Come forward, Mazzy," Ma–Tas–Kah smiled, scratching Hoover behind the ear again. Mazzy didn't hesitate as she stood before the old man, who handed Hoover to her. "You have a calm spirit, which is why animals are drawn to you."

Hoover scurried into Mazzy's sweatshirt as the old man laid his glowing hand on her head.

"Your spirit emblem is the raven," he said. "Calm

and insightful of the world far below."

Mazzy staggered a few steps and fell down near Austin. Jackson saw Hoover pop his head out of the pocket for a moment and disappear back inside.

Jackson looked up at Ma–Tas–Kah, who stared back him with a gentle smile. "I sense a deep river of wisdom flowing through you, Jackson," he said. "You see things others ignore, and that is a characteristic of a great leader."

Ma–Tas–Kah waved Jackson toward him. Jackson stood before him, but the old man motioned for him to stand next to him, which he did. Ma–Tas–Kah wrapped his arm around his shoulder. The hair on the back of Jackson's neck stood up. He felt power coming from the old man.

"You have so much good in you, Jackson," the old man whispered. "So for that, I will give you the most sacred of animal totems–the bison."

Before he knew what was happening, Jackson felt energy surge through his veins. He tried to ask the old man a question, but he found that he couldn't. He tried to move, but he couldn't get his body to respond. He was frozen as Ma–Tas–Kah gave him his animal totem.

Jackson felt shadows creeping up around him, and darkness filled the edges around his vision.

"Jackson, you must dig down deep and find the strength that you and your friends will need to defeat the Sta–au," Ma–Tas–Kah said. "Only by standing together and fighting together will you have a chance of vanquishing them for good."

Jackson had never passed out before, but he knew he was going to now. He felt like a balloon being filled with too much air that was going to pop. He felt like whatever the power the old man was filling him with was going to rip him apart. His knees buckled and he knew he was only seconds away from unconsciousness.

Jackson concentrated with all his might and forced himself to talk. "How... will... I... know... what... to... do?"

Ma–Tas–Kah lifted his hand off Jackson and all the light disappeared in the cavern. It was pitch black. Before Jackson crumpled in a heap, he heard the whisper from the old man drift to his ears. "You'll know when the time comes."

Jackson collapsed to the ground, unconscious.

The wolf and raven emerge

CHAPTER ELEVEN
Powers

Jackson awoke to someone screaming his name.

"Jackson, say something!" Austin yelled. "Jackson, can you hear me?"

Jackson opened his eyes, but couldn't see anything. It was as dark as if his eyes were still closed.

"I'm here."

"Jackson, where are you?" Austin asked.

"He's right next to you, Austin," Mazzy said.

"Where? I don't–"

Austin's flying arms hit Jackson on the back of the head.

"Ouch!"

"Oh, there you are," Austin said, relieved. "What happened?"

"I don't know," Jackson said, rubbing the back of his head. "Where's Ma–Tas–Kah?"

"He's gone," Mazzy said. "The altar is gone, too."

"How do you know?" Jackson asked.

"Because I'm looking at where he sat, and he's not here anymore," she said.

Jackson got to his feet. He put his arms out in front of him and felt around so he wouldn't run into anything. "Mazzy, can you see in here?"

"I can see perfectly. Why? Can't you?"

"It's pitch dark," Austin said.

"We can't see anything," Jackson said.

"Well, why can I see then?" Mazzy said.

"It must be because of your animal totem," Jackson said. "Don't ravens have incredible eyesight?"

"Yeah, I guess," Mazzy said.

"You're going to have to lead us out of

here," Jackson said.

Jackson felt Mazzy grab his hand and lead him forward a couple of steps, and then felt her place Austin's hands on his shoulders.

"Okay, guys, I'll get us out of here," Mazzy said.

Jackson was surprised, but the walk back to the mouth of the cave didn't seem to take as long as the walk into the cave. They hadn't traveled far before Austin said, "I see light up ahead."

And sure enough, just a little while later, Jackson saw the glow of daylight up ahead. When they stepped outside, it had stopped raining, and patches of blue sky poked through the clouds.

"How long were we in there?" Austin asked.

Jackson looked over at Mazzy as Hoover spotted a butterfly and jumped out of her pocket to chase after it. Mazzy stepped forward to try and catch her furry friend when her foot snagged on a tree root and she tumbled forward. Jackson grimaced, preparing for Mazzy to smack down hard on the ground. But to their surprise, Mazzy didn't hit the dirt. In fact, her entire body floated five inches in the air.

"Oh–" Austin said.

"My–"Jackson said.

"Gosh!" Mazzy laughed.

Jackson and Austin, mouths hanging open, stared at their friend hovering above the ground.

"You can fly!" Austin said. "That's so cool!"

"I don't think you can call this flying," Mazzy smiled. "I'm floating."

"Well, whatever it is, it's really cool," Jackson said. "Try moving, Mazzy."

"How?" she said.

Jackson and Austin squatted down next to her. Austin ran his hand back and forth in the empty space between her body and the ground. Jackson hesitated, but he finally got the nerve to nudge her shoulder with his finger. Mazzy giggled as she glided ever so slightly to her right.

"Push me harder!" she pleaded.

Using both hands, Austin shoved Mazzy as hard as he could. She shot forward, flying as easily as a bird across the hillside.

"Wow," Austin said, "she's moving pretty fast."

Right then Jackson noticed the grove of trees directly in front of her. She didn't see them, and, even if she did, he didn't know if she could stop before crashing into them.

"Look out, Mazzy!" Jackson screamed. "There are—"

Before he could finish warning her, Jackson felt something shoot forward in a blur, kicking up dirt and gravel in its wake.

"What was that?!" Jackson asked, turning to look at

Austin. But Austin wasn't anywhere to be seen.

Jackson looked at Mazzy again and couldn't believe his eyes. Austin had somehow managed to run ahead and stop her before she flew into the trees. Mazzy apparently could control where she flew, because she lifted off the ground and circled around Austin, who decided to test his newfound speed and zipped around the mountain meadow faster than Jackson could follow him with his eyes.

Mazzy, smiling from ear-to-ear, flew back over to Jackson. Her feet touched down on the ground as soft as a feather.

"Did you see Austin run?" she asked. "I've never seen anything move that fast."

Jackson felt a sudden rush of air and saw Austin standing in front of them.

"I can't believe it!" Austin said. "I set out running to try and stop Mazzy from flying into trees, and before I could even blink, I was standing in front of her."

"It's amazing!" Jackson said. "I can't believe it either."

"What can you do, Jackson?" Mazzy asked.

"Yeah, try and do something," Austin said.

"What do I do?" Jackson asked.

Austin and Mazzy both shrugged their shoulders.

"Well, how did you two discover your powers?" he asked, anxiously.

"I don't know," Mazzy said. "I tripped, then the next thing I knew I was floating."

"Yeah, I didn't even really think about it," Austin added. "It just kind of happened."

They stared at him, waiting for him to do something miraculous. Jackson wanted to discover his new power, but had no idea how to do it.

"Just try to fly," Mazzy urged.

Jackson took a running step and tried jumping into the air, but he landed back on the ground with a jolt. He tried it again, but he got the same result.

"I don't think I can fly like you, Mazzy," Jackson said, as he turned to look at her.

Austin stood next to Mazzy, but in the time it took to blink, he stood next to Jackson.

"Try running super fast like me," Austin suggested.

Jackson set off running across the mountain meadow as fast as he could. No matter how hard he concentrated, he couldn't run any faster than he normally did. He stopped in the middle of the meadow, out of breath, sweating, and realizing he was covered in mud. Mazzy flew over to him.

"You must just have some other power," she said.

"Yeah, it must be something else," Austin said, coming to a screeching stop right next to them.

"It makes sense that your spirit totem of a raven would give you the power of flight, Mazzy," Jackson said. "And wolves are fast, Austin. But what power comes with the spirit totem of the bison?"

Austin and Mazzy both turned and looked off in the same direction at the same time. They both looked concerned. Austin lifted his head and sniffed the air.

"Something's burning," Austin said. "Do you guys smell that?"

Jackson sniffed, but all he could smell was the recent rain. "I don't smell anything."

"We've got to get back to camp," Mazzy said. "Right now."

"But we don't know which way camp is, right?" Jackson asked, looking at his friends.

Mazzy pointed in the direction she looked. "It's that way."

"Are you sure?" Jackson asked.

"Yes," said both Mazzy and Austin as they both turned to look at Jackson.

"We've got to hurry," Mazzy said.

"Something is wrong back at camp," Austin said.

Jackson understood what they wanted to do. "Go ahead. I'll catch up."

Austin winked and streaked off, kicking up patches of soil behind him. Mazzy put a hand on Jackson's shoulder.

"Are you sure you'll be okay finding your way back to camp?" she asked.

"I'll be fine," he said. "Go find out what's wrong."

Mazzy smiled as she floated into the air,

disappearing above the tree line.

Jackson, alone in the meadow, ran in the direction his friends had gone. He followed Austin's tracks in the mud. He hoped nothing too bad was happening back at camp, but if the knot in his throat was any indication, that wasn't going to be the case.

Evil is afoot

CHAPTER TWELVE
The Battle

Jackson's lungs burned, his legs ached, and his hands were scraped and bloody from pushing aside shrubs and tree branches as he headed toward camp. He'd been running for what seemed like hours when he saw the black plume of smoke billowing into the late afternoon sky. He wondered what was burning as he continued onward.

Skidding to a stop, he looked down into the valley, but couldn't believe what he was seeing. The Blackfoot Braves Society Summer Camp was in flames! Without giving it a moment's thought, Jackson charged down the hill and into camp.

Up ahead, he saw Austin zipping around Bill in a blur. Bill seemed to be thrown slightly off balance, nearly dropping the torch in his hand. Jackson ran toward them, but suddenly, without warning, Bill threw a punch, sending Austin flying off his feet and crashing to the ground.

Bill ran off, frantically scratching himself, leaving Austin shaken on the ground. He rubbed the back of his head as tried to get his bearings.

"Austin, what's going on?" Jackson said, helping Austin on his feet.

"A Sta–au has possessed Bill," Austin said. "He's setting the camp on fire."

"What?" Jackson asked. "How do you know it's a Sta–au?"

Austin dusted himself off. "Couldn't you see how he was scratching himself? It's just like Ma–Tas–Kah said."

Jackson looked around the camp for any sign of Mazzy. "Where's Mazzy?"

"The last I saw of her, she was trying to put out the

fires," Austin said. "Go find her and help, and I'll try to stop the Sta–au who has Bill."

Austin raced off in the direction Bill had gone. Jackson turned and headed toward the nearest burning bunkhouse. Jackson circled around it, but he saw no sign of Mazzy. Right before he was going to move to the other burning building, he stopped dead in his tracks. Not looking where he was going, he had nearly fallen into the enormous fire pit Bill must have dug while they were gone. It was supposed to be for the bonfire celebration tomorrow night. Jackson carefully walked around the pit, but right as he turned the corner, he was splashed with water from above. He looked up and saw Mazzy floating as close to the flames as possible while she dumped a large bucket of water on the fire.

"Mazzy, down here," Jackson yelled.

She drifted down to the ground next to him. "It's the Sta–au."

"Austin told me," he said. "He's trying to stop the

one that's possessed Bill."

"Help me try to put out the fires," Mazzy said. "He used gasoline to start them, so the flames are really hot."

She floated just above the ground over to a hose that was fed by water from a well. There were five other buckets that were all empty.

"Keep filling up the buckets," Mazzy said. "I'll dump them on the fire."

Mazzy struggled to fly with a sloshing bucket of water up over the bunkhouse that was now engulfed in flames. Jackson filled the rest of the buckets as Mazzy dumped the water directly onto the fire. She drifted back down, dropping the empty bucket and picking up another filled with water.

Jackson continued filling the buckets until he felt something warm on his neck. He turned around and came face to face with a snarling grizzly bear. Jackson didn't know bears could get that big. It was enormous. He saw rotten flesh in between the animal's razor-sharp teeth. It was so

He saw rotten flesh in between the animal's razor-sharp teeth.

close, Jackson could see its eyes were black as coal and its breath was hot and rank.

"Jackson, don't move," Mazzy said.

He sensed Mazzy hovering over his head, but Jackson couldn't take his eyes off the bear growling in his face. The beast kicked up its back leg and frantically scratched its underbelly, groaning as it did so.

"It's a Sta–au," Jackson muttered to himself.

Out of the corner of his eye, he saw Mazzy float around the bear, trying to get the animal's attention.

"Hey, bear, up here!" she shouted, clapping her hands together. "Look at me!"

With a guttural roar, the animal stood on its hind legs, towering over Jackson by several feet. Jackson couldn't move. He knew this was it. The animal was going to come crashing down on him and that would be that. The Sta–au would trample him to a pulp.

The bear came down, lunging toward Jackson with its teeth bared. In a final act of defiance, Jackson balled his hand into a fist and threw a wild punch, connecting with the beast's muzzle.

Everything seemed to stop, and Jackson heard crickets singing off in the distance. He watched the enormous bear topple to the ground, out cold.

Jackson looked up at Mazzy, who floated above the enormous beast. Her mouth hung open as she looked from the bear to Jackson and back again.

"What did you do?" she asked.

"I don't know," Jackson said, shrugging his shoulders. "I punched it."

Mazzy landed on the ground next to him. "You knocked out a bear with one punch."

"Yeah, I guess I did."

"How'd you do that?"

Jackson raised his hands in an "I don't know" gesture.

"You're one tough cucumber," she said, feeling his bicep.

It felt like all the blood in Jackson's body rushed to his face.

"I guess we know what power comes with the spirit totem of the bison," she said. "Strength."

Jackson and Mazzy stepped back from the bear as they heard a loud whirring noise coming from the beast. They both watched in disbelief as a small, serpentine black cloud rose out of the bear. The mini tornado picked up momentum and moved off the bear to the ground. Jackson rubbed his eyes, but he distinctly saw a set of glowing eyes staring out from the apparition. Jackson took a step toward it, but it whisked off in a flurry, disappearing into the forest.

"Did you see those eyes too?" Mazzy asked.

"It was a Sta–au," Jackson said.

Right then the bear groaned, and its front paw twitched.

"Is the Sta–au still in that thing?" Mazzy yelled.

The bear opened its eyes, and Jackson saw they looked normal now that the Sta–au had left the animal's body.

"No, the bear is just waking up," Jackson said, ushering Mazzy away. "Let's get out of here before it comes to."

As they ran around the corner of the building, Austin flew through the air, slamming against the side of the bunkhouse. Mazzy and Jackson helped him to his feet.

"Austin, what happened to you?" Mazzy asked.

Mazzy and Jackson followed where Austin pointed his shaky finger. They saw Bill, holding a sledgehammer, walking toward them. His eyes looked like solid black marbles devoid of any human expression. The Sta–au twirled the sledgehammer above his head, preparing to bring it down on Austin.

Right as the sledgehammer was inches from smashing into Austin's head, Jackson lifted his hand and caught it easily. The Sta–au, momentarily confused, stared at Jackson, who ripped the sledgehammer out of its hands and flung it away as hard as he could, sending it off into the treetops.

The Sta–au threw its head back and howled a blood-curdling yell that sent a shiver down Jackson's spine. Out of the corner of his eye, he saw two funnel clouds making their way toward them. Jackson got to his feet and shoved Bill as hard as he could, sending him crashing to the ground directly in the path of the funnel clouds.

Jackson helped Austin to his feet and turned to Mazzy. "Get Austin out of here. I'll deal with the Sta–au."

"How?" Mazzy asked.

Jackson didn't want to hurt Bill.

"I'll think of something. Now go."

Mazzy helped Austin as they rushed away as fast as they could go.

Jackson turned around just as the two small, black tornados merged, forming a larger tornado cloud that slowly disappeared inside Bill's body. It caused his body to bulge like a balloon being filled to the point of bursting. Jackson stood his ground as Bill lumbered toward him.

In a voice that sounded more like an animal than a man, Bill said, "Ma–Tas–Kah chose you as one of his warriors? A child? Ha! The old man grew tired of waiting, it seems."

"What do you want?" Jackson asked, hoping he wouldn't be forced to hurt his favorite camp counselor who was possessed by demons.

Bill's body seemed like it was on the verge of exploding as it took feeble steps toward Jackson. "We want every last one of you dead, and we'll not stop until that day!"

Jackson took a step toward the lumbering Bill. "Well,

I plan on stopping you."

The Sta–au howled with glee. "You can't stop us, child. Nobody can!"

Jackson used all his strength and shoved Bill's body, but it felt like he was trying to push a mountain. Bill smacked Jackson, sending him flying through the air and landing on the ground with a thud. Jackson saw stars and his ears rang. He forced himself to stand up.

Jackson glanced over his shoulder as he backed away from Bill. He was nearing the fire pit, and he suddenly had an idea.

"Ma–Tas–Kah was right," Jackson said, "the Sta–au are weak and feeble, nothing to be worried about."

Jackson heard the rumbling of rage gurgling deep within Bill.

"He told us that we shouldn't fear you," Jackson said, carefully gauging his distance to the fire pit. "We should pity you."

Bill rolled his head back and howled at the night sky.

Jackson hoped his words would make the Sta–au angry, and it looked like they were.

"Come on, you filthy beast," Jackson shouted. "Come get me."

Bill lumbered forward, charging full speed toward Jackson. Right as he was nearly upon him, Jackson jumped aside and watched as Bill toppled to the bottom of the fire pit, landing with a thud.

Jackson looked down as the Sta–au that possessed Bill tried to crawl its way out of the pit, but it was no use–it was too deep. It was trapped.

Suddenly, Bill stopped trying to get out. He looked like he was momentarily stunned. Before Jackson knew what was happening, the camp counselor stumbled back, falling to the ground. Jackson heard a hissing sound as he watched a black mist rise out of Bill's body, which deflated back to its normal size. The mist formed into a tornado and Jackson could swear he saw a snake's face in the cloud hissing as it floated to the top of the pit, circled around him, and whishing off into the forest.

Jackson sighed with relief as Bill sat up, his eyes returned to their normal appearance.

"Jackson, what happened?" Bill asked, looking around the pit. "How did I get down here?"

Jackson was thinking about what to tell him, when Bill fell back down, passing out from exhaustion.

Austin and Mazzy ran up to the side and pit and looked down at Bill.

"What happened?" Austin asked.

"The Sta–au left Bill's body and took off into the forest," Jackson said.

"Is Bill all right?" Mazzy asked.

"I think so, but let's talk about this after we get these fires put out," Jackson said, running off with Austin and Mazzy behind him.

The three worked as team to put out the fires. They found that they all worked well together. After they finished, they got Bill out of the fire pit and got him to bed.

They got Bill out of the fire pit

Bill woke up a little while later and asked what had happened. He couldn't remember anything after digging the fire pit two days ago. Jackson, Austin, and Mazzy had agreed to tell him the same story.

"You must have been struck by lightning," Jackson said. "When we got back from our treasure hunt, you were lying unconscious by the fire pit."

Bill scratched his head as he thought about it. "Wow!" was all he said.

Jackson is the bison

CHAPTER THIRTEEN
Heroes

The next day, Jackson sat next to his friends in the dining hall. The rest of the camp had arrived back from the overnight hike to Granite Mountain that morning. They were exhausted, as they had been caught in the storm the day before and had gotten soaked. They came back to discover two of the charred bunkhouses from the fire the night before.

Bill addressed the whole camp. He explained that he didn't know exactly what happened, but he suspected that lightening had struck the two bunkhouses during the storm and caused the fires.

"My thanks go to Jackson, Austin, and Mazzy for putting out the flames," Bill said, pointing at them. "You should all give them a big round of applause for saving the

Blackfoot Braves Society Summer Camp."

All the boys and girls in the dining hall erupted, clapping their hands and hooting and hollering. Austin stood up and bowed dramatically. Hoover popped his head out of

Mazzy's sweatshirt to see what the ruckus was. She immediately put her hand over his head to keep the chipmunk out of sight. Jackson felt his face turn bright red from the attention.

While eating their dinner after Bill finished his speech, Craig walked over and leered down at Austin and Jackson.

"I don't care what Bill said," Craig sneered. "I bet you geeks had something to do with setting those fires."

Jackson and Austin looked up at Craig with expressions completely devoid of concern for what he'd said. They both went back to eating their dinners. This seemed to infuriate Craig, who plopped his hands down on the table in front of them.

"Did you hear what I said?!" Craig yelled.

"Yes," Jackson said, "but as you can see, we don't really care what an ignorant bully like you chooses to believe."

Craig lifted his right hand, balled it into a fist, and threw it at Jackson's face. Craig watched in disbelief as Jackson caught his fist in his hand and held it firmly as he finished chewing his mouthful of food.

"Leave me and my friends alone, or we're going to have a serious problem," Jackson said, tightening his grip ever so slightly on Craig's hand. Jackson knew he wasn't seriously hurting Craig, but it was very satisfying to see the look of surprise from the bully. Apparently Craig was not accustomed to being overpowered by anyone, much less a smaller victim of his ruthlessness. Jackson let go of his fist.

Craig nursed his hand as he sulked back over to his friends.

Jackson went back to eating his dinner as Austin

chortled. "That was hysterical," Austin laughed. "These powers are going to come in handy."

Jackson smiled, but he knew their powers were meant for so much more. The Sta–au were still out there somewhere, and Jackson knew they were going to come after Ma–Tas–Kah's three warriors. That was certain.

But next time, Jackson, Austin, and Mazzy would be ready for them.

THE END

gunnison county
Libraries
connect.   discover.   imagine.   learn.
Gunnison Library
307 N. Wisconsin, Gunnison, CO 81230
970.641.3485
www.gunnisoncountylibraries.org

ABOUT THE AUTHORS

THE WRITER:
CHRISTOPHER E. LONG

Christopher lives in Southern California with his wife, Jamie, and their son, Jackson. He writes comic books, childrens novels, and screenplays, and he can't think of anything else he'd rather do.

THE ARTIST:
MICHAEL GEIGER

Michael has created storyboards for NBC and TNT television features, sketch layouts for Kevin Costner, and concept art for video games published by Eidos, Ubisoft, and Sony. He'd rather do what Christopher does.

ACKNOWLEDGEMENTS

**Christopher would like to thank
his parents, James and Cheryle,
who believed in him when
no one else did.**

**Michael would like to thank
Shannon and Patrick for being
his first official publishers in print.**

Creative Direction and Editor: Shannon Denton
Book Design and Production: Patrick Coyle

Special thanks to John Helfers,
Aron Lusen, and Hope Aguilar.

The publishers wish to thank Dakota,
Katherine, Kristen, and Wyatt for their
continued support and inspiration, and
Byron Preiss for his belief in our vision.

The text type for this book is set in Baskerville.
The display type is Mesquite.
The illustrations are pencil and digital ink.

Author's Disclaimer

The Story in *Blackfoot Braves Society: Spirit Totems* is a work of fiction. I took artistic license with elements in the story for entertainment purposes. The Blackfoot people have a heritage rich with music, ceremonies, and customs.

To learn more about them and their history, please visit:

www.blackfoot.org

or visit your local library.

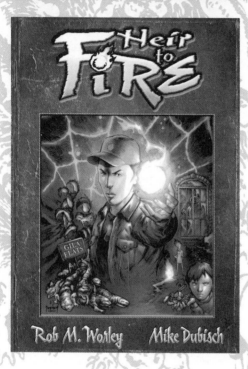